ROBOT RESCUE!

Don't miss any of the cases in the Hardy Boys Clue Book series!

HARDY BOYS

➤ Clue Book ◄

#13

ROBOT RESCUE!

BY FRANKLIN W. DIXON ⟷ ILLUSTRATED BY SANTY GUTIÉRREZ

ALADDIN

NEW YORK   LONDON   TORONTO   SYDNEY   NEW DELHI

ALADDIN

An imprint of Simon & Schuster Children's Publishing Division
1230 Avenue of the Americas, New York, NY 10020
First Aladdin hardcover edition April 2021
Text copyright © 2021 by Simon & Schuster, Inc.
Illustrations copyright © 2021 by Santy Gutiérrez
Also available in an Aladdin paperback edition.
All rights reserved, including the right of reproduction in whole or in part in any form.
ALADDIN and related logo are registered trademarks of Simon & Schuster, Inc.
THE HARDY BOYS and colophons are registered trademarks of Simon & Schuster, Inc.
HARDY BOYS CLUE BOOK and colophons are trademarks of Simon & Schuster, Inc.
For information about special discounts for bulk purchases, please contact
Simon & Schuster Special Sales at 1-866-506-1949 or business@simonandschuster.com.
The Simon & Schuster Speakers Bureau can bring authors to your live event.
For more information or to book an event contact the Simon & Schuster Speakers Bureau
at 1-866-248-3049 or visit our website at www.simonspeakers.com.
Series designed by Karina Granda
Jacket designed by Tiara Iandiorio
The illustrations for this book were rendered digitally.
The text of this book was set in Adobe Garamond Pro.
Manufactured in the United States of America 0321 FFG
2 4 6 8 10 9 7 5 3 1
This book has been cataloged with the Library of Congress.
ISBN 9781534453371 (hc)
ISBN 9781534453364 (pbk)
ISBN 9781534453388 (eBook)

CONTENTS

AUTOMATION SENSATION

"A robot that makes ice-cream cones?" eight-year-old Joe Hardy exclaimed. "This I've got to see!"

"Seeing is believing," Joe's nine-year-old brother, Frank, said.

"And so is *tasting*!" their best friend, Chet, declared.

Frank, Joe, and Chet had lots to be excited about that spring Friday afternoon. They were on their way to Bayport's newest ice-cream parlor—Robo Freeze!

"It's so cool that you won that ice-cream-eating

contest at the mall, Chet," Frank said. "Thanks to you, we'll get a sneak peek at Robo Freeze before it opens tomorrow."

"A sneak peek plus a sneak *lick*!" Chet replied. "Sherbot makes ice-cream cones, remember?"

"How could we forget?" Joe asked, grinning.

Sherbot, the ice-cream-making robot, was the creation of the Andersons, a family of inventors living in Bayport. It had been their idea to open an ice-cream parlor on Bay Street where all cones were scooped by Sherbot!

The three boys couldn't wait to check out Robo Freeze before the grand opening. But as they neared the store, they saw a small group of kids gathered outside. Some of them were holding signs.

"Don't they know Robo Freeze doesn't open until tomorrow?" asked Frank.

"I don't think they *want* Robo Freeze to open at all," Joe said, pointing down the street. "Check out their signs!"

As they neared the group, the brothers and Chet read some of the messages:

ICE CREAM—NOT NICE CREAM!

ROBO? OH NO!

ROBOT = RUST BUCKET!

"Definitely not Sherbot fans," Frank stated.
"They're fans of Len and Barry ice cream,"

Chet explained. "My sister, Iola, is president of the fan club."

"Len and Barry?" Joe asked. "You mean the guys who sell ice cream from a tie-dyed truck?"

"You mean the *best* ice cream," Iola said, approaching the boys. "Len and Barry invented the awesome flavor Bubble Gum Yum, you know."

"Bubble Gum Yum isn't my favorite," said Chet, shaking his head. "I mean, do you chew it or lick it?"

Iola rolled her eyes as if to say, *Seriously?*

Frank pointed at the sign Iola was holding, which read DEPROGRAM ALL ROBOTS! "I know you like Len and Barry's ice cream, Iola, but what do you have against robots?"

She turned to two other club members. "Mason, Gabriela, tell them."

"An ice-cream-making robot will take customers away from Len and Barry," Mason explained.

"Soon robots will replace everybody," Gabriela said. "Even teachers."

"Robo teachers?" Joe joked. "Can they be programmed not to give homework?"

"Very funny," said Iola, but she didn't laugh. "I thought you guys were detectives, not comedians."

Frank and Joe *were* detectives, who loved solving mysteries more than anything. The boys even had a notebook where they figured out the five *Ws* of each new case: *Who*, *What*, *Where*, *When*, and *Why*.

Iola led the club in a chant to close down Robo Freeze. Their voices were soon drowned out by a jingly tune played by a truck pulling up to the curb—the Len and Barry ice-cream truck.

Len leaned out of the truck's window and shouted, "Peace out, kids! Ready for a far-out surprise?"

Barry appeared at the window, holding a tray of tiny cups filled with ice cream. "Sample the new flavor we whipped up just for you," he said. "We named it Fan Club Grub!"

"Omigosh! Fan Club Grub?" Iola said excitedly. "They named a flavor after us?"

The club members tossed their signs in a pile on the sidewalk, then raced toward the Len and Barry ice-cream truck.

"I wonder how it tastes," said Frank.

"I like all of Len and Barry's flavors except one,"
Joe said, shuddering. "Lickety-Split Licorice!"

"Don't tell that to Iola," Chet warned. "The Len
and Barry Fan Club loves every flavor the guys have
ever made."

"That's cool," Joe said with a smile. "But you know
what's even cooler? Trying ice cream made by a *robot*!"

The brothers and Chet approached the Robo Freeze entrance. The window shades were down and the door was locked.

"Let's try this," Frank said, ringing the doorbell.

After a few seconds, the door opened halfway. A boy poked his head out. Frank, Joe, and Chet recognized him as ten-year-old Holden Anderson. Holden went to a private school for kid geniuses in the next town.

"Hi," Chet said. "I'm Chet Morton, the winner of the ice-cream-eating contest—"

"I know who you are," said Holden. "Quick, what's the secret password?"

"What secret password?" Chet groaned. "I didn't know I needed a secret password to get in!"

"Chet, just make one up," Frank murmured.

"The password is . . . marshmallow!" Chet guessed.

"Good enough," said Holden as he flung the door wide open. "Are you ready to meet Sherbot, the man of the hour?"

"Don't you mean *can* of the hour?" Joe joked. "After all, he *is* a robot!"

That earned Joe an elbow-nudge from Frank.

"No more robot jokes, okay?" Frank whispered. "The Andersons take their work very seriously."

Frank, Joe, and Chet followed Holden inside Robo Freeze. Each wall of the ice-cream parlor was painted a different color: orange, blue, yellow, and red. Silver and red café tables with matching chairs were set up, ready for customers the next day.

"Hey, look!" Frank said, pointing toward the back of the store. Behind the counter, with a huge round head, a cheery smile, and flashing green eyes was—

"That's got to be Sherbot!" Joe declared.

"The one and only!" said Holden proudly.

Chet and the Hardys rushed to the counter to get a better look. They were so busy checking out the robot, they hardly noticed Mr. and Mrs. Anderson standing behind the counter too.

"Guys, meet my parents," Holden said. "They built and programmed Sherbot, and I helped with coding."

"Holden is a *microchip* off the old block!" Mr. Anderson joked. "Right, Phyllis?"

"Right, Steve." Mrs. Anderson chuckled. "Our name may be Anderson, but we're thinking of changing it to *Androidson*!"

While the Andersons laughed it up, Joe whispered to Frank, "No robot jokes, huh?"

"Mom, Dad, this is Chet," said Holden. "He's the winner of the ice-cream-eating contest."

"Thanks for inviting me and my friends for a sneak lick—I mean, sneak peek—at Robo Freeze," Chet said.

"You'll get to sample Sherbot's ice cream too," Mr. Anderson said. He pointed to a row of jumbo cardboard boxes standing against the yellow wall. "We didn't stock up on all those for nothing."

"What's in the boxes?" Joe asked.

"Crunchy sugar cones," Mrs. Anderson said with a smile, "waiting for Sherbot to fill them with delicious ice cream."

Chet was busy studying a chalkboard on the wall. Listed there were fifteen different flavors.

"How does Sherbot know what flavors to fill the cones with?" he asked.

"Sherbot runs by voice commands," Holden explained. "All you have to do is tell him."

"Take a crack at it, Chet," Mr. Anderson said. "Order the first official cone from Sherbot."

"Just start with the command that makes Sherbot come to life," said Mrs. Anderson. "It's 'Sherbot, make my ice cream.'"

Chet stepped up to the counter. "Sherbot, make my delicious, mouthwatering, lip-smacking ice cream!"

Sherbot's green eyes kept flashing as his head began to swivel back and forth. With a whirring noise, the robot faced Chet. "Greetings," he droned. "Name your consistency. Scoop or soft serve?"

"Scoop, please," Chet replied. "Make it a double."

Sherbot's robotic left hand lifted a cone. He faced the icebox and droned, "State your flavor clearly, please."

"You've got so many, it's hard to choose," Chet said, looking up at the chalkboard. "But I really like chocolate."

"Chocolate. Affirmative," Sherbot said, grabbing an ice-cream scooper with his other hand. He was

about to dig into a tub of chocolate ice cream when Chet blurted out, "Wait! I like banana rocky road, too. But I also *really* like almond fudge crunch. Not as much as peppermint candy, but only if it has real chunks of peppermint—"

"Cease commands! System overload!" Sherbot droned as his green eyes flashed rapidly and his arm waved the scooper through the air. "Begin again. Begin again. Begin again—"

"What did I do?" Chet asked.

"Sherbot is programmed to take one command at a time, Chet," Mr. Anderson said. "Why don't your friends get their cones while you decide on a flavor?"

"I'll go next," said Joe. "I know what flavor I want."

Chet stepped back as Joe took his place at the counter.

"Sherbot, make my ice cream," Joe commanded. In response to the robot's questions, he ordered one big scoop of mint chocolate chip.

"Mint chocolate chip. Affirmative," Sherbot declared.

Frank, Joe, and Chet watched wide-eyed as the big gleaming robot landed a flawlessly round scoop of mint chocolate chip ice cream in a sugar cone.

"Is Sherbot the perfect robot or what?" exclaimed Holden.

Still holding the ice-cream cone, Sherbot coasted toward the toppings bar. "Name your toppings, please," he droned.

"That's easy," Joe said. "Make it hot fudge."

Sherbot ground to a halt. "Negative. Command not recognized."

"Sherbot hasn't been programmed to squeeze hot fudge yet," Mr. Anderson explained. "We're working on it."

"No hot fudge?" Chet complained. "How perfect can an ice-cream-making robot be if he doesn't rock hot fudge?"

"Sherbot is perfect!" Holden insisted. "Why don't you ask for whipped cream instead, Joe?"

"Whipped cream," Sherbot droned. "Affirmative!"

The robot placed the ice-cream cone inside a holder. He then grabbed a can, pressed his robotic fist on the top, and—

PFFFFFFIIIITTTT! A torpedo of white cream shot over the boys' heads. Behind them, a voice shouted, "Cheese and crackers!"

Frank, Joe, and Chet spun around to see a woman wearing a blue uniform and apron, with a blob of whipped cream on the front of her hairnet. The boys recognized her at once. She was their school lunch lady, Mrs. Carmichael.

"Oops," Joe whispered. "Bad aim!"

Chapter 2

SURPRISE IN STORE

Standing next to Mrs. Carmichael was the brothers' friend Phil Cohen. What was he doing there?

"Mrs. Carmichael?" asked Frank.

"You were expecting Dolley Madison?" Mrs. Carmichael growled. She pulled her apron up to wipe her forehead, then said, "There will be no food fights. Not in my clean lunchroom!"

"Um . . . Mrs. Carmichael?" Phil said. "We're not in the school lunchroom now. We're in Robo Freeze."

"So there'll be no food fights in Robo Freeze!" Mrs. Carmichael snapped. "I hate food fights wherever they are!"

"We're sorry for Sherbot's whipped-cream slipup, Mrs. Carmichael," said Mrs. Anderson.

"Thankfully, it's an easy fix," Mr. Anderson said. "We just have to code Sherbot's arm to aim lower, that's all."

"You do know that Robo Freeze doesn't open until tomorrow," said Mrs. Anderson. "Don't you?"

"I'm not here for an ice-cream cone with sprinkles," Mrs. Carmichael said. "Tell them why we came, Phillip."

Phil threw back his shoulders. "We came for Sherbot's specs!"

Frank and Joe traded looks. A robot's specs meant how it was built to work.

"I want my school lunchroom to have its own ice-cream-making robot," Mrs. Carmichael explained. "Simple as that."

Joe gasped. "An ice-cream-making robot in our lunchroom?"

He reached for his mint chocolate chip ice-cream cone—with no whipped cream—and gave it a lick.

"That would be awesome," said Frank.

"Better than awesome—it's a dream come true." Chet closed his eyes, thinking about the possibility. "And I dream a lot about ice cream!"

"What makes you want a robot for your school lunchroom, Mrs. Carmichael?" Mr. Anderson asked.

"I'm tired of serving ice cream and frozen yogurt to dozens of kids every day," Mrs. Carmichael explained. "By the time I'm finished scooping and squirting all those icy treats, the chicken nuggets and hush puppies are ice cold too!"

She pointed across the counter. "That's why I want a robot just like your Sherbot. I like that he's smiling, too, so I don't have to."

"Building a robot isn't easy," said Holden. "Have you ever built one before, Mrs. Carmichael?"

"No, but Phillip here has," Mrs. Carmichael said, giving him a smile. "He's won several science fairs, so he's the kid for the job."

While Mrs. Carmichael admired Sherbot, Joe whispered to Phil, "Are you really going to build Mrs. Carmichael a robot?"

"She promised me mac and cheese every day for the rest of the year if I helped her," Phil whispered back. "What would you do?"

"I'd build ten robots for mac and cheese," Chet whispered. "No-brainer."

Mrs. Carmichael turned to the Andersons. "So let's discuss Sherbot's specs," she said. "I can give you something tasty in exchange. How does a month's supply of frozen meat loaf sound?"

"I'm sorry, Mrs. Carmichael," Mr. Anderson said gently. "I'm afraid our specs for Sherbot are top secret."

Mrs. Carmichael's eyes didn't blink for at least five seconds as she stared at the Andersons. "Top secret?" she finally exclaimed. "Okay—I'll throw corn dogs into the deal!"

"Sorry. The only way to find out how Sherbot works would be to open him up," Mrs. Anderson added. "And I know you wouldn't do that, Mrs. Carmichael."

"She definitely doesn't know Mrs. Carmichael," Chet murmured to Frank and Joe.

"I heard that, Chet Morton!" Mrs. Carmichael snapped. "No extra ketchup on your burgers from now on."

"Phooey," Chet grumbled.

Mrs. Carmichael frowned at the Andersons. "No specs, huh? Well, this is a pretty kettle of fish sticks."

Phil was frowning too. And then his expression slowly shifted into a smile. "Don't worry, Mrs. Carmichael," he said. "I just thought of a way to get your ice-cream-making robot."

As Phil left with Mrs. Carmichael, the brothers wondered what he'd meant, but their thoughts were interrupted when Mr. Anderson called out, "Who's next for ice cream?"

The boys were about to reply when the door opened again. This time Cecil Mortimer and his son, Milford, walked in.

Frank and Joe knew that the Mortimer family lived in one of the biggest houses in Bayport.

Six-year-old Milford got whatever he wanted—and what he wanted was a lot!

"We're next, I believe," Cecil declared.

"I'm sorry," Mr. Anderson told them. "Robo Freeze doesn't open until tomorrow."

"I'm afraid that would be too late," Mr. Mortimer said. "Milford's birthday party is tomorrow, and we need your robot to make a large ice-cream cake."

"Sherbot doesn't make ice-cream cakes," Mrs. Anderson said. "Only delicious ice-cream cones."

Milford pointed to Sherbot. "Then I want an ice-cream-making robot for my birthday party, Dad! He can make ice-cream cones for everybody!"

"But Milford," said Mr. Mortimer, "I thought you wanted a pony to give your little friends rides."

"Not unless the pony has a big round head and makes ice-cream cones," Milford insisted. "I want an ice-cream-making robot, and I want him now!"

"Come along, Milford," Mr. Mortimer said, leading his son out the door. "I'll make sure your birthday party tomorrow is perfect. I promise."

With the Mortimers gone, Sherbot started making an ice-cream cone for Frank. But when it was Chet's turn . . .

"I'll pass, thanks," Chet said. "Ice cream isn't ice cream without hot fudge."

"But—" Holden started to say before his dad piped up.

"We'll have Sherbot squeezing hot fudge in no time, Chet. Don't give up on Robo Freeze yet."

Frank, Joe, and Chet thanked the Andersons, then filed out of the ice-cream parlor.

"Chet, since when do you turn down ice cream?" asked Frank, then took a lick of his vanilla ice-cream cone with rainbow sprinkles.

"Since Len and Barry are still giving out free samples." Chet pointed to the ice-cream truck still parked at the curb.

"They're for the fan club," Joe reminded him. "And you're not a member."

"I may not be a member of the fan club," Chet said with a grin, "but I am a humongous fan of their ice cream!"

As he walked toward the truck, he called out, "A double scoop of Fan Club Grub, please—with gobs of hot fudge!"

Still eating their cones, Frank and Joe started the walk home.

"Let's go back to Robo Freeze tomorrow for the grand opening," Joe suggested. "I want to take a video of Sherbot in action."

"Great idea," said Frank. "An ice-cream-making robot is history in the making."

"Sherbot can make history," Joe said between licks of his almost-finished mint chocolate chip. "As long as he keeps making awesome ice cream."

Saturday morning Frank and Joe returned to Bay Street. There was already a big group gathered outside Robo Freeze.

"Wow," Frank exclaimed. "It looks like all the kids in Bayport are excited to see Sherbot!"

"So am I," Joe said, patting his pocket. "I borrowed Dad's phone to make a video of him."

He and Frank squeezed into the crowd. The store

was supposed to open at eleven, and it was already eleven fifteen.

"Maybe they're unpacking more cones," Frank suggested.

After another ten minutes, impatient kids began to shout, "We want Sherbot! We want Sherbot!"

The door finally opened and the Andersons filed out. None of them were smiling. Not even Holden. *What was up?*

"Uh . . . hi, kids," Mr. Anderson called out. "Thanks for coming to the big opening, but Sherbot can't make ice-cream cones today."

"No ice cream?" a girl in the crowd shouted.

"Did Sherbot break?" a boy called out.

"He didn't break!" said Holden, stepping forward. "Sherbot can't make ice cream today because . . . because . . . *he's gone!*"

Frank and Joe exchanged confused looks. Had Holden just said *gone*? Gone where?

Chapter 3

BOTNAPPED!

Mr. Anderson called out above the puzzled voices. "Thank you all for coming. As soon as we find Sherbot, Robo Freeze will be open for business."

Forcing a smile, Mrs. Anderson added, "As our Sherbot was programmed to say . . . have an *ice* day!"

The Andersons went back into the store. It didn't take long for the disappointed crowd to break up and leave the scene.

"Let's find the Len and Barry truck," one girl said.

"I'll bet their ice cream is better than a robot's, anyway," her friend grumbled.

Frank and Joe stood staring at Robo Freeze's door. Sherbot was missing. And to detectives, missing meant business!

"Frank, do you think Sherbot walked out of the store?" Joe asked. "By himself?"

"Maybe. Let's go inside and see what we can find out."

The door to Robo Freeze was closed, but not locked. Frank and Joe slipped inside and looked around. What they saw made their mouths drop open. Not only was Sherbot gone from the counter, the surrounding walls were streaked and splattered with mush!

Joe gasped. "Holy guacamole!"

The Andersons stood on one side of the store, their faces grim with worry.

"Not guacamole," said Mr. Anderson. "Marshmallow, butterscotch, and strawberry. Ice-cream toppings."

"As if poor Sherbot put up a fight!" Mrs. Anderson wailed. "Before he was . . . botnapped!"

"Botnapped," Frank repeated. "So you think Sherbot was taken?"

"Of course Sherbot was taken," Holden said. "Our robot was programmed to make ice cream, not unlock a door, open it, and take a hike!"

"Okay, so when did you first notice that Sherbot was missing?" asked Joe.

Mr. Anderson pointed to the staircase at the back of the ice-cream parlor. "We live in the apartment above the store," he explained. "When we came down early this morning, Sherbot was gone."

"Did anyone call the police?" Frank asked. "A missing robot is serious."

The Andersons all shook their heads, their eyes wide.

"We don't want to tell the police," Mr. Anderson replied. "You see, I'm embarrassed that I forgot to lock the front door last night."

"The robot rustler could have walked right in," said Mrs. Anderson.

Joe gazed around at the trashed ice-cream parlor. "If you all live above the store, didn't you hear any noises downstairs?"

"We're deep sleepers." Mr. Anderson sighed. "We don't even hear each other snoring."

Mrs. Anderson wrung her hands nervously. "We have to find our Sherbot, but where do we start?"

Joe flashed Frank a look that said, *I thought they'd never ask!* "Mr. and Mrs. Anderson, start with us!"

"Joe means we're detectives," Frank explained. "We're pretty good at finding missing things."

"But you're just kids," said Mr. Anderson.

"Kid *detectives*," Joe pointed out. "Mysteries are our name. *Who*, *what*, *where*, *when*, and *why* is our game."

"Detectives, huh?" Holden said softly while his parents traded weary looks.

"Oh, go ahead, boys," Mr. Anderson finally told Frank and Joe after a long silence. "Have fun playing detective."

"In the meantime, we're closing down the store," said Mrs. Anderson sadly. "What's Robo Freeze without Sherbot?"

The Andersons began picking up the napkin and spoon holders that had fallen off the counter. Frank and Joe walked around the tables and chairs toward the door.

"*Play* detective. Give me a break," Joe mumbled. "And I never even got to take a video of Sherbot."

He stopped suddenly and pulled the phone from his pocket.

"Sherbot's not here," Frank said as Joe began scanning the wrecked ice-cream parlor with the phone camera. "What are you filming?"

"The crime scene," replied Joe with a smile. "And the answer to one of the five Ws. *Where* the crime took place."

The Andersons were now too busy scrubbing the walls with paper towels to notice Joe filming the store from top to bottom, side to side.

Once outside, Joe replaced the phone in his hand with something he never left home without—the boys' clue book. "Let's get to work," he said, opening the book and pulling out the pencil tucked inside.

Frank watched as Joe wrote on the top of a clean page: *Who's Got Sherbot?* Underneath, he wrote the five Ws. Next to *where* he wrote, *Robo Freeze*.

Who's Got Sherbert?
What? Robot disappeared
When? by night/early morning
Where? Robo Freeze

Why?

"Now that we figured out *where*," Joe said, "*what* happened?"

"All we know so far is that someone took Sherbot out of Robo Freeze," Frank replied.

"*When* was probably during the night or early in the morning," Joe added. "The Andersons said they came downstairs this morning and Sherbot had already vanished."

After listing *when*, it was time for the only *W*s left—*who* and *why*. Frank and Joe knew that figuring out one often led to the other.

"*Who* would want to take a huge robot out of an ice-cream parlor?" Joe wondered out loud.

"Someone who wants an ice-cream-making robot," Frank said. "Someone like Milford Mortimer."

"Milford really wanted Sherbot to make ice-cream cones at his birthday party," Joe pointed out. "And what Milford wants, he usually gets."

"Maybe his dad got him Sherbot," Frank suggested. "He did promise Milford the perfect birthday party. We heard him with our own ears."

While Joe started their suspect list, writing down Milford's name, Frank asked, "Who *wouldn't* want an awesome ice-cream-making robot?"

Wouldn't? Joe grinned as a new thought clicked into place. "Iola Morton and the Len and Barry Fan Club are not fans of Sherbot!"

"They didn't want Sherbot to take customers away from Len and Barry," said Frank. "So maybe they took Sherbot instead!"

Joe added the Len and Barry Fan Club to their suspect list. "Two suspects are a good start. Who should we question first?"

"I say Milford Mortimer. If only we could go to his house and look for Sherbot."

"Good luck with that," Joe said with a snort. "That fancy house has a high gate and a guard outside."

He was slipping the clue book into his pocket when—

"Out of our way, out of our way!" a voice shouted.

Frank and Joe whirled around to see six-year-old twins Matty and Scotty Zamora hurrying up the sidewalk. Each boy pulled a bright red wagon piled high with boxes from Pizza Palace, their parents' pizza parlor on Bay Street.

"What are you guys doing?" asked Joe.

"What does it look like we're doing?" Matty snapped as the pair took a break from wheeling. "We're delivering pizzas!"

"That many pies?" Frank asked. "Who could eat that many?"

"These pizzas are for Milton Mortimer's birthday party," Scotty said with a smile, "at the biggest house in Bayport!"

Frank and Joe traded wide-eyed looks. Had Scotty just said *Milton Mortimer's* house?

Chapter 4

PARTY ANIMAL

"So that's where all those pizzas are going," Joe said. "Were you invited to the party?"

"We were," Matty said with a frown, "but we have to go back to Pizza Palace right after we deliver these pies."

"How come?" Frank asked.

"Mom and Dad need our help." Scotty sighed. "They want us to twist garlic knots with our sister, Daisy."

Matty shook his head. "The high school kid who works at Pizza Palace on Saturdays is home with a cold," he wailed. "How could he do that to us?"

The twins started sulking away with their wagons.

"Wait!" Frank shouted. "Why don't we deliver the pizzas for you?"

Joe smiled when he figured out his brother's plan. "Sure! If you start twisting garlic knots now, you'll still have lots of time to go to Milford's party after you finish."

Matty and Scotty let the wagon handles drop to the ground. After trading high fives with Frank and Joe, they turned back toward Pizza Palace.

"Thanks, Hardys!" Matty called over his shoulder. "Tell Milford to save us some birthday cake."

"We'll save him some garlic knots!" Scotty added.

Frank and Joe picked up the wagon handles and began wheeling the pizza boxes toward the Mortimer mansion.

"That was some good thinking, Frank," Joe said. "With this pizza delivery, we can get into Milford's house and look for Sherbot."

"Let's just hope we can get past the guard!" said Frank.

A little while later, the brothers stopped their pizza wagons in front of the Mortimer gates, where a guard stood blocking their way. The badge on her uniform read ROBERTA.

"Oh, the pizzas are here," she said smiling. "I'll call Mr. Mortimer to come out to collect them."

The brothers froze. That wasn't their plan. They'd have to think fast. . . .

"Um, we're not just regular pizza delivery guys," Joe said. "We're *singing* pizza delivery guys!"

"Yeah. It's our job to sing 'Happy Birthday' to Milford Mortimer," added Frank. "The whole song."

Roberta raised an eyebrow. "I was told there'd be a pizza delivery, not a *singing* pizza delivery, but okay. You can go in."

"Yes!" Joe cheered, then quickly added, "Thank you, ma'am. We appreciate it."

Roberta pressed a button to open the gate. "The party is in the backyard," she said. "Go around the house and you can't miss it."

The house was enormous, so wheeling the wagons around it to the back took longer than the brothers thought it would. When they finally reached the backyard—

"Whooooaaaaa!" Joe cried.

Frank gasped. "Roberta was right. Who could miss all this?"

Spread across the lawn were huge, colorful bouncy castles. Circling one castle was a bouncy moat filled with inflatable sea monsters and dragons.

On one side of the yard, Frank and Joe spotted Milford dressed in a king's robe and crown. While the birthday boy sat on a gold-colored throne, his friends sat on the grass. They all watched two armored knights battle with plastic swords. Mr. and Mrs. Mortimer stood side by side watching too, their backs to the Hardys.

"I think the theme of this party is King Arthur's court," said Frank.

"You mean *King Milford's* court!" Joe joked. "Let's unload the pizzas and look for Sherbot."

After stacking the pizza boxes on a snack table, the Hardy brothers parked the wagons underneath.

Then they set off on their quest to find Sherbot.

Milford and his guests were too busy watching the knights to notice Frank and Joe sneaking through the yard.

"Wow, check out the birthday cake!" Joe exclaimed.

Frank followed Joe's gaze. Set up on another table was a huge cake decorated to look like a knight's sword and shield! "That cake's awesome, but I don't see Sherbot making ice cream around here."

"Maybe the party's not ready for ice cream yet," Joe said. "Maybe Mr. Mortimer has Sherbot hidden as a big surprise!"

Frank looked around the huge lawn. "Hidden where?"

Joe wasn't sure. And then something across the yard caught his eye. "There!" he exclaimed, pointing.

Frank watched his brother race toward a small silver trailer. Painted across its side was a big letter *S*.

"*S* for *Sherbot*, Frank!" Joe called. "And it's sure big enough to hold a robot!"

"Don't open it, Joe," shouted Frank as he ran after his brother. "We don't know what's inside!"

But Joe was already opening the trailer door.

When he looked inside, he didn't see a robot. Instead a small brown pony stared back at him. He gave a snort, shook his mane, and let out a loud *neighhhhh!*

Joe stepped back as the pony hoofed its way out of the trailer. Milford's friends pointed and shouted as the pony galloped around the yard.

"Is that the pony for my party?" Milford called out. "It's my birthday, and I want to keep him. I want that pony!"

Milford's parents watched the pony with wide eyes. Mrs. Mortimer covered her mouth with her hand to keep from screaming.

"Why is Sapphire out?" Mr. Mortimer demanded.

The pony stopped before the dessert table. After another snort, he began munching on the creamy shield-shaped cake.

"I don't want him anymore!" Milford said angrily. "He's eating my birthday cake!"

"That's because it's a carrot cake, Milfy," said Mrs. Mortimer. "Horses love carrots."

"Then I don't want the cake, either," Milford said with a frown. "I wanted chocolate!"

The knights tried coaxing the pony away from the table, but they didn't seem to be having much luck. Neither did Frank and Joe.

"You boys over there," Mr. Mortimer called. "Did you let the party pony out of his trailer?"

Joe gulped. "Um . . ."

"Er . . . ," Frank began.

What they really meant was . . . *busted!*

Chapter 5

TRUCK STOP

Frank and Joe trudged over to Mr. Mortimer, heads hanging. They had nothing to say but the truth.

"Sorry," Joe said. "I let Sapphire out of his trailer when I was looking for something else."

"What could you possibly have been looking for out here?" cried Mr. Mortimer.

"For Sherbot, the ice-cream-making robot," Frank answered. "He's been missing since early this morning."

Mr. Mortimer's brows flew up with surprise. "You mean that robot Milford and I saw yesterday at Robo Freeze? Why would he be here?"

"Because Milford really wanted Sherbot for his birthday party," Joe explained. "And since he mostly gets what he wants . . ."

"Uh, Joe," Frank interrupted, his voice low. "I don't think Sherbot is here."

Joe turned to stare at Frank. "Why not?"

"Because Milford got *them* instead."

Joe looked to see where Frank was pointing. In the distance stood a man and woman dressed in court jester costumes. The bells on their caps jingled as they flipped scoops of ice cream over each other's heads and under their legs into cones.

"Wow!" Joe exclaimed.

Next, using two cones, the woman juggled four scoops in the air. After the ice cream landed precisely—two scoops in each cone—she bowed and handed the cones to a guy wearing a cowboy hat.

Frank and Joe were so amazed by the ice-cream acrobats, they didn't notice Milford standing behind

them. "Let's see Sherbot do that!" he sneered. "Who needs an ice-cream-making robot when you can get the famous Scooper Dupers for your birthday party?"

Mr. Mortimer pointed at the cowboy now licking both ice-cream cones. "And there's the pony wrangler who *should* have been watching Sapphire."

Joe turned to Frank and said, "You're right. Milford wouldn't need Sherbot if he had the Scooper Dupers. They're pretty awesome."

"The Mortimers don't have Sherbot," Frank decided. "Let's get Matty's and Scotty's wagons and keep investigating."

"Wait!" Milford called out. "How did you get into my party, anyway? I didn't invite you."

"We delivered pies from Pizza Palace," Joe replied. He nodded toward the snack table. "The pizzas that Sapphire is busy eating."

The Mortimers gasped as Sapphire nudged a pizza box open to nibble on the pie inside.

"I hope he likes pepperoni," said Frank.

Milford's friends laughed and shrieked as Mr. and Mrs. Mortimer and the cowboy charged toward Sapphire. While they tried gently to pull the pony away from the pizzas, the brothers slipped under the table to grab the wagons.

The Hardys wheeled the wagons out of the yard and away from the house. "That was the biggest birthday party I ever saw!" said Frank.

"And that pony really takes the cake!" Joe joked.

Frank and Joe returned the wagons to Pizza Palace. Matty and Scotty had just left for Milford's party. They also left the brothers six garlic knots for delivering the pies.

"I was hoping for pizza," Joe admitted as they carried the knots to their favorite booth by the window, "but it's lunchtime and my stomach is growling like a dinosaur!"

After finishing lunch, Joe crossed Milford's name off the suspect list. "Our only suspects left are the members of the Len and Barry Fan Club."

"Should we question them next?" Frank asked.

Joe looked out the window and pointed to a tie-dyed truck parked outside. "I have a better idea. Why don't we question Len and Barry first?"

The brothers left Pizza Palace and headed straight for the truck. Len and Barry weren't at the window, but Frank and Joe could hear them loud and clear inside.

"Dude," Len said. "Our fan club came through for us again."

"Totally," Barry replied. "That robot idea of theirs was excellent!"

The Hardys turned.

Robot idea?

ICE-CREAM SCHEME

"Did you hear what they said?" Frank hissed.

"Yeah," Joe whispered back. "Something about a robot—"

Len and Barry suddenly appeared at the window.

"Hi, guys!" Len boomed with a big smile.

"What flavor can we get you?" asked Barry.

"Thanks, but we're not here for ice cream today," Frank said. "We're here for answers."

"You guys said something about a robot," said Joe. "What was that all about?"

Len and Barry stared at the brothers, their smiles melting away.

"Um . . . you must have heard the word 'rabbit,' not 'robot,'" Barry said. "Unfortunately, we're out of Hoppity Hazelnut."

"Like, bummer, right?" Len forced a chuckle.

Frank and Joe knew what they'd heard, and it definitely wasn't "rabbit."

"Thanks, anyway," Frank said.

"Try us again, guys!" Len called after the brothers as they walked away from the truck. "We're working on a tie-dyed flavor."

"It'll be called Hippie Dippy Drippy!" Barry shouted.

The moment Len and Barry were out of earshot, the brothers discussed what they'd heard.

"Those guys were talking about the club's excellent robot idea, Frank," Joe said excitedly. "Maybe the idea was to take Sherbot."

"The club *was* worried that an ice-cream robot

would take customers away from Len and Barry. But wouldn't the fans have to know code to get Sherbot to leave the store?"

"Sherbot runs on voice commands," Joe reminded Frank. "Anyone can say 'Sherbot, follow me.' The question is, follow them where?"

"Iola is the president of the fan club. Why don't we ask her?"

When the Hardys reached the Mortons' house, they found Chet sitting on the front doorstep. Their friend's shoulders were drooping, and he hung his head.

"What's up, Chet?" Joe asked.

"You look miserable," added Frank.

"That's because I am!" Chet said, slumping down even more. "Iola is up in her room with the Len and Barry Fan Club. They've got a whole cooler of ice cream, and they won't let me in!"

"Why not?" Frank asked.

"They're up to something secret." Chet sighed. "Go upstairs and ask her yourself."

Frank and Joe went inside. After saying hello to Mr. Morton, they headed up the stairs.

"Chet said the fan club was up to something secret," Joe whispered. "I wonder if the secret is stealing Sherbot from Robo Freeze."

Iola's room was right next to Chet's. After Frank knocked, the door opened a crack and Iola peeked out. When she saw it was Frank and Joe, she opened it wider.

"Hi. Chet's downstairs."

"We know," said Frank. "We want to talk to you."

The brothers looked past Iola's shoulder into the room. The other club members were gathered there, their eyes focused on Frank and Joe.

"So, can we come in?" Joe asked when Iola didn't move.

"Not today, guys," she said. "We're super busy."

She was about to shut the door when Joe blurted out, "Wait! We're here because we want to join the Len and Barry Fan Club!"

"We do?" Frank murmured.

"Now can we come in, Iola?" asked Joe.

The other club members crowded around Iola at the door. After some whispering among the club members, she turned back to Frank and Joe. "We thought you liked that robot Sherbot's ice cream better."

"We did like Sherbot's ice cream," Joe said quickly. "But that was before we found out he didn't do hot fudge."

"No hot fudge?" Mason exclaimed.

"Len and Barry have hot fudge," Gabriela said. "And cold fudge and lukewarm fudge too."

"Exactly!" Joe said with a smile. "Which is why Len and Barry rule!"

"Can we come in and join now?" Frank asked.

"Maybe," said Iola. "First you have to pass a test."

Frank and Joe traded looks as they followed Iola into the room. *Test? What kind of test?*

"All members have to pass a taste test," Iola explained as she pointed to a big cooler set against one wall. "You have to be able to identify any of Len and Barry's flavors without looking."

Mason opened the cooler to reveal half a dozen clear plastic containers inside.

"This is my kind of pop quiz!" Joe declared. "Bring on the scoops!"

"I guess that means you'll go first," Iola said to Joe. "Blindfold him, Mason."

Joe smiled while Mason tied a bandanna over his eyes. He and Frank hadn't planned on joining the fan club, but if it meant answers and free ice cream, he was all in!

"Joe, we'll give you spoonfuls of Len and Barry's ice cream, one at a time," Iola said. "You must identify four out of five flavors to become a member of the fan club."

"Piece of cake," Joe said, smirking. "*Ice-cream* cake."

"This is serious," said Iola. "We're about to begin."

"Good luck, Joe!" Frank called.

Joe couldn't see a thing, but he felt a spoon being placed in his hand. Raising it to his mouth, he tasted the first flavor.

"It's . . . Marshmallow Mud Pie!" he blurted out.

"Correct!" Iola said.

Joe sampled the second, then the third.

"Moo-Moo Igloo . . . and Lip-Smacker Cracker!"

"Yes and yes!" Iola said. "You have one more to go."

"You can do this, Joe!" Frank cheered.

Joe grinned with confidence as he raised the fourth spoon to his mouth, but when he tasted the ice cream, he wished he hadn't.

"Blech!" he shouted. "This is Lickety-Split Licorice! Yuck!"

"Great." Frank groaned. Of all flavors, they had to stick in the one that made Joe gag!

Iola stared, horrified, as Joe sputtered. "How can you be a fan of Len and Barry if you hate Lickety-Split Licorice?"

"Are you sure you want to join this club?" asked Gabriela. "Or maybe you're spies for Robo Freeze."

Joe pulled off his blindfold just as Chet ran through the door. "Iola, the Len and Barry truck is outside!" he said excitedly. "They told me they want to speak to you guys right now!"

"Seriously?" Iola said. She turned to the other members. "This sounds super important. Let's go!"

The members of the fan club charged to the door, but just as they reached the hallway, Iola cried, "Wait! We can't leave the secret formula!"

Secret formula?

Mason raced back to Iola's desk. He tore a piece of paper from a pad sitting there and shoved it into his pocket, then darted out the door.

Chet groaned. "At last. I thought they'd never leave!"

"Why is the Len and Barry truck outside?" Frank asked.

"The truck's not out there," Chet admitted. "I was trying to get rid of them." He grinned as he crossed the room to the cooler. "Now I can have all this awesome ice cream for myself. Like Lickety-Split Licorice, my favorite!"

Joe tried hard not to gag as Chet dug into the charcoal-gray ice cream. While Chet feasted, the brothers discussed what they'd just seen and heard.

"Mason took a secret formula," Frank said. "Maybe it has something to do with Sherbot."

"But Mason tore it off the pad," said Joe. "We'll never know what was on that piece of paper."

Frank hurried over to Iola's desk. After studying the pad, he said, "That's what you think."

Joe joined Frank at the desk. Looking down at the pad, he asked, "What do you mean? All I see is a blank page."

"Look closer," said Frank. "The top sheet doesn't

have any writing, but it does have scratches on it from the last note."

"You mean from what was written before?" Joe asked.

"Watch." Frank picked up a pencil and scribbled over the scratches with the side of the point. Words appeared like magic.

"Way to go, Frank," Joe exclaimed. "Now we can read the secret formula!"

Chet had already moved on to the next flavor as Frank and Joe deciphered the message.

"'Nuts, marshmallows'?" Frank read out loud. "'Shredded coconut'?"

"'Pretzels, dried peaches'?" Joe read. "Frank, what kind of secret formula is this?"

SHOP TILL YOU DROP!

"This is stuff to eat," Frank said. "Could their top secret formula be a recipe?"

Joe pointed to the top of the page. "There are some scratches you forgot to draw over," he said.

Frank used the pencil to make more words appear. "It says, 'End Effector Nectar.' What's that?"

"Chet, what's an End Effector Nectar?" Joe asked their still-snacking friend. "Do you know?"

"Nope," Chet mumbled through a full mouth.

"An end effector is a robot's hand," a girl said from behind them. The boys looked over to see Iola leading the others back into her room. The entire club looked disappointed.

"You made us go downstairs for nothing, Chet," Iola said, narrowing her eyes. "Len and Barry weren't outside."

"They weren't?" Chet asked. "Oops."

A club member named Raphael pointed to the brothers standing at Iola's desk. "Hey, look!" he said. "That's our secret recipe!"

"But I tore off the secret recipe," Mason insisted. He looked at Frank and Joe. "How did you do that?"

"A little detective magic," Joe admitted. "So we could find out if you had Sherbot."

"Sherbot the ice-cream-making robot?" asked Iola. "Why would we have him?"

"The Len and Barry Fan Club was protesting Robo Freeze yesterday," Frank said. "You were worried that kids would buy ice cream from Sherbot instead of Len and Barry."

"We *were* worried," Iola admitted, "but we would never steal anything. Especially a robot."

"Then what's this top secret recipe all about?" Joe asked.

Mason nodded proudly. "It's a new Len and Barry ice cream flavor!" he said. "We invented it ourselves."

"It was Len and Barry's idea," Raphael said. "They didn't like that we were mad at Robo Freeze."

"Len and Barry wanted us to do something nice instead," added Gabriela. "They challenged us to invent a new flavor to celebrate robots, not protest them."

"And we came up with End Effector Nectar!" Iola declared.

"Cool," said Frank. "But why is it top secret?"

"We e-mailed the recipe to Len and Barry," Iola explained. "They like it so much they want to keep it secret until the big reveal next week."

"They say it'll be bigger than Moo-Moo Igloo!" Mason said. "How awesome is that?"

There were high fives all around as the club

members celebrated their ice-cream success. Frank believed that they hadn't taken Sherbot and didn't have him hidden somewhere. But Joe still wasn't sure. . . .

"How do we really know you guys didn't take Sherbot last night?" he asked. "You were mad that robots were taking human jobs."

"Guys, they couldn't have been at Robo Freeze last night," Chet said. "They were here in the house all night coming up with their robot flavor."

"They were?" asked Joe.

"Sure," Chet replied. "Their sleeping bags are still in the basement, if you want to see for yourself."

Joe groaned. "Chet, why didn't you tell us before?"

"You didn't ask!"

Iola folded her arms across her chest. "Now do you believe us?" she asked the Hardys.

Joe nodded and said, "Yeah. And your robot flavor is safe with us."

"Good." Iola pointed to Chet, who was digging

into a container of Very Merry Strawberry. "The problem is, no flavor is safe with my brother!"

"Should we pick up ice cream for dessert?" Fenton Hardy asked as he pushed a shopping cart down the frozen foods aisle.

Remembering his run-in with Lickety-Split Licorice a few hours before, Joe shook his head. "No thanks, Dad. Let's have fruit salad instead."

"A nice healthy choice," said Laura Hardy. "Your dad and I will get the fruit while you guys find that cereal you like."

"On it, Mom," Frank said. He and Joe took the cart and walked quickly up the aisle. But as they turned the corner—

WHAM! They crashed right into their friend Phil.

The collision knocked the shopping bags from Phil's hands, spilling their contents all over the floor. The brothers looked down at an ice-cream scooper, an apron, spoons, and a package of plastic dessert cups.

"Sorry, Phil," Joe said. "Are you taking some kind of cooking class?"

"No," said Phil. "It's for a project I'm working on."

"We'll help you pick up the stuff," Frank offered.

But when he lifted a packaged hairnet, Phil snatched it out of his hand. "I've got it, thanks. I'll see you in school on Monday."

"Okay," Frank said.

"See you," added Joe.

As they made their way to the cereal aisle, Joe turned to Frank. "Did you see that?" he asked in a whisper. "Phil was buying a hairnet."

"So?"

"So," Joe replied, grinning, "I just remembered who *else* wanted Sherbot!"

Chapter 8

LUNCHROOM DOOM

"Remember? Mrs. Carmichael wanted Sherbot's specs so Phil could build a matching robot for our lunchroom," Joe said as they turned down the cereal aisle.

"We heard Phil tell Mrs. Carmichael that he thought of a way to get her a robot," Frank said. "I wonder if that meant taking Sherbot."

"Would Phil do all that for Mrs. Carmichael?" asked Joe.

"Probably not," Frank decided. "He might do it

63

for a whole year of mac and cheese, though. He said so himself."

The brothers stopped at a cereal shelf. As they looked for the brand they liked, Joe said, "Phil is an awesome inventor, but do you think he could build a new robot that quickly?"

"No . . . unless Phil turned Sherbot into an ice-cream-scooping lunch lady," replied Frank. "Hair-net, apron, and all."

"In that case, we *have* to save Sherbot."

"Let's go to Phil's house tomorrow and look for the missing robot right after we have breakfast."

Joe reached up and pulled their favorite cereal off the shelf. "Did someone say breakfast?"

The next morning the brothers headed straight for Phil's house to look for Sherbot. Joe had already added Phil's name to their suspect list.

When no one answered the doorbell, Frank and Joe walked around the house to the backyard. Phil's inventor workshop was inside a small shed.

"Maybe we'll find Phil in there," said Frank.

"Or, even better," Joe said, "maybe we'll find Sherbot!"

In the backyard, Mrs. Cohen was planting gladiola bulbs in her garden.

"Hi, Mrs. Cohen," Joe called.

"Is Phil in his workshop?" asked Frank.

Mrs. Cohen pushed back her sun hat. "Phil went to school today, guys."

"On a Sunday?" Joe asked.

"He's working on a special project," Mrs. Cohen explained. "Something for Mrs. Carmichael, the lunch lady, but he didn't tell me what."

Frank and Joe traded sideways glances. *Mrs. Carmichael, huh?*

The brothers thanked Mrs. Cohen, then practically sprinted all the way to Bayport Elementary School a few blocks away.

"If Phil is with Mrs. Carmichael," Joe said excitedly, "maybe Sherbot is there too!"

On Sundays, the school was open for kids who wanted to use the gym and for special clubs. When the guard, Mr. Altman, saw Frank and Joe, he grinned. Mr. Altman knew all the kids at school by name.

"Well, if it isn't the Hardy brothers," he boomed. "Don't tell me they have a special detective basketball game here on Sundays!"

"No, Mr. Altman." Joe chuckled.

"We're looking for our friend Phil Cohen," said Frank.

"And a big robot!" Joe added. "Have you seen them?"

"I didn't see Phil today," Mr. Altman said. "And I think I would have noticed a big robot entering the school."

"I guess," Joe sighed.

Mr. Altman stepped aside to let the brothers through the door. "Go on in and ask around, boys. Maybe the kids in the gym know where Phil is."

Frank and Joe thanked Mr. Altman before heading inside. They walked up the empty hall, not sure what to do next.

"Too weird, Frank," Joe said. "Mrs. Cohen said Phil came here today to meet Mrs. Carmichael."

A thought popped into Frank's head. He turned to Joe. "Doesn't the lunchroom have a big back door for special deliveries?"

"Yeah," said Joe. "So?"

"*So* if a robot isn't a special delivery," Frank said, "I don't know what is!"

The brothers hurried to the lunchroom. The double doors were shut, but they heard a voice coming from inside—a robotic-sounding voice droning, "State your order . . . state your order, please."

"Frank," Joe said excitedly, "I know a robot voice when I hear one, and I know I hear Sherbot!"

Frank nodded. "We're going in."

The brothers burst through the double doors into the lunchroom. They didn't see Mrs. Carmichael or Phil. They did see something else. Something that made their jaws drop. . . .

Behind the lunch counter, a robot with flashing blue eyes stood decked out in an apron, with a hairnet around his head. On top of the counter sat a huge steel pot.

"State your order." The robot whirred as his

head turned to the right, then the left. "One meatball or two . . . ? No extra sauce . . . Keep the line moving, please."

"That robot is not Sherbot, Joe," Frank pointed out. "And he's not serving ice cream."

"I thought I smelled meatballs," Joe said. "Let's get a better look."

The brothers walked toward the counter, but halfway there—

FWUMP!

The two of them yelped as a big ropy net dropped down from the ceiling over them.

"Ahhh!" Joe shouted. "Mrs. Carmichael's got us trapped—under a *giant hairnet*!"

MEAT-BRAWL

Frank and Joe wrestled with the giant net, trying to get out from under it.

They heard someone say, "That's not a giant hairnet."

It was a voice the brothers knew well. They peeked out from between the ropes. Phil was standing off to the side.

"If it's not a giant hairnet," Joe asked, "what is it?"

"It's what Mrs. Carmichael uses to drop balloons from the ceiling on the last day of school," Phil said, walking over to help them untangle themselves. "My next project is to fix it so the net doesn't drop too."

"I guess you still have some work to do," said Frank. "Can you get us out of here, Phil?"

Phil helped the brothers find the edge, and then the trio dragged the net to the side of the lunchroom.

"What's that robot behind the counter?" Joe asked.

"That's Lunchbot," Phil said with a grin. "Pretty cool, huh?"

"Not if you took Sherbot apart to build him," Frank said.

"Take Sherbot apart?" asked Phil, surprised. "Why would I do that?"

"Mrs. Carmichael wanted a robot just like Sherbot," Joe replied. "When she couldn't get Sherbot's specs, you said you had another way of getting her an ice-cream robot."

"I did," Phil admitted. "But Sherbot had nothing to do with it."

Phil walked behind the counter to Lunchbot's side. "I took a robot I made for a past science fair," he explained, "then reprogrammed him into a lunch-serving bot."

While Phil adjusted Lunchbot's apron, the brothers whispered to each other.

"He's telling the truth, Frank," Joe said. "I recognize that robot from a science fair Phil entered last fall."

"What did the robot do?" Frank asked.

Joe shrugged. "I can't remember."

"It doesn't matter what the robot did before. Lunchbot serves meatballs!"

Frank and Joe turned to see Mrs. Carmichael right behind them. Even on a Sunday, she was wearing her lunch lady uniform, apron, and hairnet.

"Why meatballs, Mrs. Carmichael?" asked Frank.

"We thought you wanted a robot to scoop ice cream so you didn't have to," Joe added.

"That was my initial plan," Mrs. Carmichael admitted. "But after I thought about it, I'd rather serve the fun foods like ice cream for a change."

She pointed to the robot. "Lunchbot here will take care of the chicken nuggets, fish sticks, carrots and peas, and meatballs. In fact," she added, "I came to school today to make meatballs so Phil could test his robot out."

"So you didn't want a robot like Sherbot?" Frank asked.

"No," Mrs. Carmichael replied. "Why should I

only be popular on mac and cheese day?" She smiled at Phil. "Which for Phillip will be every day, thanks to his hard work."

Phil pumped his fist and cheered. "Yes!"

Frank leaned closer to Joe. "I think I believe Mrs. Carmichael."

"Me too," Joe replied in a quiet voice.

"What are you boys whispering about?" Mrs. Carmichael demanded. "You're not planning a food fight for Monday, are you?"

"No, Mrs. Carmichael," Frank said quickly.

"We would like to see how Lunchbot works, though," said Joe.

"It's too soon, guys," Phil admitted. "I haven't tried out the voice commands yet."

"So try them out now, Phillip," Mrs. Carmichael said, giving him an encouraging smile. "Give 'im a whirl!"

"Okay," Phil said, sticking a pair of metal tongs in the robot's fist. "Who wants to order the first meatballs?"

"I do," Frank offered.

"And since I never got to film Sherbot," Joe said, pulling out his dad's phone, "I'll film *Lunchbot* instead."

Phil directed Frank to step in front of Lunchbot. The moment he did, the robot droned, "How many meatballs? State your order clearly."

"I'll have two meatballs, please," Frank said.

Lunchbot began to whir. Instead of using the tongs to grab meatballs, he dropped them to the floor with a clatter.

"What's he doing?" Mrs. Carmichael cried.

Lunchbot stuck his robotic hand into the big pot of meatballs. He leaned all the way back and hurled a jumbo meatball over Frank's head!

Mrs. Carmichael and the boys watched the juicy meatball whiz across the lunchroom and hit the opposite wall with a *SPLAT*! Everyone ducked as Lunchbot began hurling more and more meatballs across the lunchroom!

"There goes my awesome mac and cheese deal!" Phil groaned.

"And I just remembered what your robot did at

the science fair, Phil," Joe said, ducking again. "He pitched softballs!"

An angry Mrs. Carmichael pointed at Lunchbot. "I don't care if you're a robot," she shouted. "There'll be no food fights in my lunchroom!"

Phil commanded Lunchbot to stop flinging while the brothers raced out the back door.

"We didn't see that coming," Frank said once they were outside. "At least we got to rule Phil out as a suspect."

"And I got to film Lunchbot," Joe said. "And I managed to do it without getting meatball mush on the phone."

The brothers watched Joe's video of Lunchbot hurling meatballs. They had to agree that a meatball-pitching robot was pretty funny.

"What's not funny is that we're out of suspects," Joe said. He was about to put the phone away when Frank stopped him.

"We never watched your crime-scene video of Robo Freeze. We may not have any more suspects, but we still might spot clues."

Joe pulled up the video of Robo Freeze and hit play. He and Frank saw the splattered walls and the napkin and spoon holders, which had been knocked from the counter. As the front of the store came into view, Frank said, "Stop! Pause the video there, Joe."

"Why?" Joe asked as he froze the frame.

"If the botnapper took Sherbot out through the

front door"— Frank pointed at the screen—"why weren't the tables and chairs near the door knocked over?"

Joe studied the video. He saw what Frank meant. There wouldn't have been enough room to move a big robot between the tables. But then Joe noticed something else. . . .

"The floor in the front of the store isn't messy either. Just in the back."

He ran the video again. This time, he hit pause when some big ice-cream-cone boxes came into view. "Why is this one box upside down?" Joe asked. "That's kind of weird."

"So is this," Frank said, pointing to the upside-down box. "A light is blinking inside the box. A *green* light. You can see the glow near the floor."

"So what does that mean?" Joe asked slowly.

Frank turned to his brother, trying to contain his excitement. "It means there's something inside that upside-down box. And it's not ice-cream cones!"

THE HARDY BOYS—and YOU!

WANT TO JOIN FRANK AND JOE IN CRACKING THE CASE OF

the runaway robot? Write your answers down on a piece of paper. Or turn the page to find out what really happened!

1. Frank is pretty sure the box with the blinking green light isn't filled with ice-cream cones. What else might be inside the box?

2. If the brothers ruled out Milford Mortimer, the Len and Barry Fan Club, and Phil Cohen, who else might know what happened to Sherbot?

3. Robots are programmed to do lots of cool things. If you could invent a robot to help detectives like Frank and Joe, what would it do? What would you call it?

Chapter 10

IN A FLASH

As Joe watched the blinking green light underneath the cardboard box, an idea popped into his head. "Weren't Sherbot's eyes green, and didn't they flash? Frank, are you saying Sherbot's inside the box?"

Frank nodded. "Maybe Sherbot was never botnapped at all. Maybe he never left the store."

"Or maybe," said Joe, his own eyes lighting up, "maybe someone hid Sherbot underneath the box. But who would have done that, and why?"

"First things first. We have to find out if the blinking light is coming from Sherbot. Put away the phone, Joe. We're going back to Robo Freeze."

Frank and Joe left the school grounds and headed for Bay Street and Robo Freeze. When they reached the store, the shades were still down. This time, the door was unlocked.

Quietly, the brothers stepped into the dark, shadowy ice-cream parlor. They didn't see the Andersons, but they did see the upside-down box. The green light was still blinking under the cardboard.

"We've got to see what's in there," Frank said.

Joe was about to lift the box when Holden Anderson jumped out from the shadows.

"Freeze!" he shouted. "And I don't mean ice cream!"

Frank and Joe stared at the silver can in Holden's outstretched hands.

"That's right," Holden said, narrowing his eyes, "I have a can of whipped cream and I'm not afraid to use it!"

"Put down the whipped cream, Holden," said Frank.

"We told your parents we'd help find Sherbot,"

Joe chimed in. "And I think we just did."

"I don't know what you're talking about," Holden said. "Why would I hide a robot that I helped build myself?"

Frank and Joe exchanged a look. They'd never told Holden someone had hidden Sherbot. Had he just admitted that he had?

Joe turned to the upside-down box. "Why don't we let Sherbot tell us what happened?"

"W-what do you mean?" Holden had turned bright red.

Joe shouted at the box, "Sherbot, make my ice cream!"

The upside-down box began to wiggle. From underneath came a whirring noise, followed by Sherbot's robotic voice: "Scoop or soft serve . . . ? Name your flavor, please. No samples. Sorry."

Holden stared at the box, then at the brothers. He forced a smile. "You mean Sherbot's been there all this time? Awesomesauce."

"I think you knew he was there, Holden," Frank said. "Why did you hide him?"

"You probably had a good reason, right?" added Joe.

Holden fixed his eyes on his feet. After a long silence, he glanced up at the Hardys, looking miserable. "I did have a good reason. But first, would you help me get Sherbot out?"

"Gladly," Joe said.

All three boys lifted the bulky cardboard box to reveal Sherbot, his green eyes blinking as his head turned from side to side and he droned, "I am still waiting. State your flavor."

Frank and Joe smiled, glad that Sherbot was okay. At that moment, Mr. and Mrs. Anderson raced down the stairs.

"We heard a ruckus in the store," said Mr. Anderson. "Is that Sherbot?"

"The real deal, Mr. Anderson," Joe declared.

"But . . . where . . . ?" Mrs. Anderson started. "Who—"

"Mom, Dad, no one ever took Sherbot," Holden said. "He was here the whole time."

"What?" both parents said in unison.

"I hid Sherbot under one of the ice-cream-cone boxes," Holden explained. "I wanted him to be perfect for opening day. When he couldn't serve hot fudge, I thought I could fix him."

"*Fix* Sherbot?" Mr. Anderson asked.

"Friday night, while you and Mom were asleep, I came downstairs to adjust his programming. But my coding caused him to go berserk. He started throwing ice cream and toppings all over the store."

"Why didn't you wake us up and tell us?" Mrs. Anderson asked gently.

"I didn't want you to know I ruined Sherbot," Holden said. "He was too big to hide outside, so I emptied a box and covered him up."

Holden's shoulders drooped. "When you thought someone stole Sherbot, I pretended to think so too."

Holden's parents stared quietly at their son. After a moment, Mrs. Anderson said, "All you had to do was ask for help."

"We all could have figured out how to make Sherbot perfect for opening day," Mr. Anderson said. "Together. When it comes to robots, this family's a team."

"Frank and I know about teamwork," Joe said with a grin. "We're a team too. A team of detectives!"

Holden turned to his parents. "You're not mad? And I can stay in genius school?"

"Of course, Holden," said Mrs. Anderson.

"Yes!" Holden cheered.

When Mr. and Mrs. Anderson heard about how Joe and Frank had solved the case, they were impressed.

But Holden still felt bad. "All those kids really wanted to see Sherbot in action yesterday." He sighed. "I ruined everything."

"Not so fast, son," Mr. Anderson said cheerily. "Now that we have Sherbot, there's still hope for Robo Freeze."

"With just some quick re-programming," Mrs. Anderson said, "Sherbot will be the maestro of marshmallows! The wizard of whipped cream! The champion of cherries!"

"The superstar of fudge sauce!" Holden declared. "When can we open again?"

Mr. Anderson pointed at a still-splattered wall.

"Not until everything is clean again, Holden," he said with a sigh. "I'm afraid Sherbot was also the master of mess!"

Just then, they heard a lively tune jingling outside. Joe smiled. That tune could only mean one thing . . . ice cream!

And a new idea!

"Opening day for the store may have to wait," Joe said, "but maybe not Sherbot's big debut."

It was late Sunday afternoon, but not too late for ice cream, as a dozen kids lined up at the Len and Barry truck.

But this time, the ice-cream-making men were not the only ones in the truck. Joining them in the window was an ice-cream-making *robot*!

"Peace out, ice-cream-loving dudes," Sherbot droned. "State your flavor, please."

Len put a friendly hand on Sherbot's robotic shoulder. "Don't forget to tell the kids about our new flavor, Sherbot!" he said. "End Effector Nectar."

"Try it with hot fudge," Barry added.

"Hot fudge affirmative," said Sherbot, his body pivoting toward the row of squeeze bottles. "Squirting about to proceed."

Joe was determined to get an ice-cream cone from Sherbot as soon as he finished writing the last two *W*s in their clue book.

"*Who* hid Sherbot was Holden Anderson. *Why*? Because he didn't want his parents to know he . . . well . . . kind of goofed."

"Now Sherbot is better than ever," Frank said, "thanks to Team Anderson."

Frank and Joe watched as Sherbot topped a double scoop of End Effector Nectar with the perfect squirt of hot fudge sauce.

"Robots really are cool, Frank," said Joe. "But, even so, I hope there's something they never, ever replace."

"What?"

Joe grinned. "Detectives like us!"